A Boy Named Wish

A Story for Young Readers Aged 7-10

Richard & Esther Provencher

InkSpotter Publishing

PUBLISHED BY INKSPOTTER PUBLISHING
163 Main Avenue, Halifax, Nova Scotia, Canada B3M 1B3
http://inkspotter.com/

Printed and bound in the United States of America by Create Space

Dedicated to

our four children and five grandchildren

Chapter 1: Foster Child

He couldn't help staring at the people beside him. The Lawrences. They were at the Children's Aid office in downtown Truro.

"Hello," the boy said, kind of shyly. It was the first time they met.

"Hi," Mister said. "My name's Joe." Then he rushed over and pumped the boy's hand. Almost scared him to death.

"Hi," the boy said back. His throat sounded dry, and his tongue was getting thick.

"Well, Mr. and Mrs. Lawrence, here he is...Edward, Edward Wilson." The Children's Aid worker looked around the room. A picture of two parents and a child hung on the wall.

The boy didn't know if he was supposed to get off his chair again or what. He already shook hands. And he already said "hi" and "hello."

Maybe he should do it again. "Hi...Hello!" Sounded sort of stupid, but if that was what they wanted.

"Edward, my name is Ann Lawrence." The lady came over and gave him a hug.

Imagine, from a total stranger. A hug. He gave her a shy hug back. Some of her hair tickled his face. Her perfume was kind of neat, too.

This was Edward's first visit with his new foster parents. It sure felt different. Why was Mister wearing a tie? It was so hot in here. His eyes moved rapidly around the room.

Edward tried not to stare at the Lawrences. He was so nervous he could only give them a sideways look. Edward pretended to be checking out the teddy bear poster on the wall. But he was really looking them over.

When you're almost nine, you learn to check things out carefully and hide your inside feelings.

Like when Edward got blamed for starting fights at school. Even if he didn't do anything, he still got blamed. After awhile, it didn't matter anymore. But he was no angel. Maybe he did deserve to be grounded.

"Edward, for heaven's sake. When are those notes from your teacher going to stop?" Grandpa Jim wore himself out nagging and worrying about him.

Grandpa couldn't come today, he was so sick. And Edward wasn't helping much, the way he was behaving lately.

Well, it served Grandpa right, in a way. Edward was the one who had to go to a foster home. He didn't know why Grandpa had to tell Children's Aid he didn't know how to handle Edward anymore.

It wasn't really fair.

Grandpa Jim looked after Edward since both parents died in a car accident when he was five.

"I don't pee the bed anymore," Edward said out loud. Oh yeah, right. Why did he say that anyway? It was stupid.

"Well, yes, that's true enough," the social worker said quickly. "Edward has made a lot of improvements these past two months since he went to live in our emergency home.

"But now, it's time to move on," she added.

"And I don't sneak all the sweets anymore," Edward said. "I'm trying really hard to be good."

He wondered if he should keep quiet. Maybe he was talking too much. Edward didn't want the Lawrences to change their minds.

He needed to go to their home. Maybe he could change so he could go back to live with Grandpa. He remembered all that "yak...yak" between Children's Aid and Grandpa. It was all about Edward.

There were so many questions.

Then all those tears from Grandpa. Lots from Edward, too. He wished with all his heart Grandpa was here right now. But he wasn't.

"We both wear glasses," Mr. Lawrence said. "You look just like me when I was your age."

"Cool," Edward answered. His eyes searched the floor for a penny. He always picked them up off the street. So he could buy peppermints.

He adjusted his glasses and looked up at Mr. Lawrence. Edward raised his head even higher. Some people thought he acted like he was stuck up when he did this.

But he wasn't.

Mrs. Lawrence was kind of pretty. Mister was sort of bald. They moved their chairs much closer to Edward.

It seemed like they were going to take a bite out of him. Instead, he answered all kinds of questions, about where he lived and how he liked school. They were sort of nosey questions.

Finally, the big one came like an arrow out of the closet. *Get a life, Edward.* He suddenly felt things crowding in around him.

"Are you ready to go today to stay with the Lawrences?" The worker watched Edward carefully as he struggled for the right words.

He thought about his answer when he played on his Nintendo at the emergency home last night. He thought about it at school this morning. And he thought about it when he got in the car to come to the Children's Aid office this afternoon.

Edward closed his eyes. Everyone was so quiet. He knew he needed a place to work things out.

He had to show his Grandpa he could really change. No more complaining at home. Or even at school. No more hitting anyone when he got angry, either.

Edward's hands scrunched up into tight balls of bone and muscle. He could hardly sit still. Then his head cleared and filled with pleasant thoughts. Yes, it was the only way.

The worker said Edward could go home for visits after a while. Grandpa Jim would like that. Edward knew it could work out. He would show everyone.

"Yes, I want to go to the Lawrences. Right away. Today."

The three adults smiled about his decision.

Edward hung his head. He thought he was letting Grandpa down by going to live with someone else.

"What's wrong, Edward?" Mrs. Lawrence asked. "We really want you to come live with us."

"Will I become your son?" There, he said it. He heard stories about Children's Aid kids never going back to their families.

That couldn't be true. Could it?

He didn't want to be adopted. Or to never go home to his Grandpa. That was his real home.

"No, Edward, we'll only be your foster parents. You'll be a foster son. How does that sound?"

Sounded okay to him. "Okay," he said slowly, his own voice sounding far, far away.

He stood up. He really felt like running away, but he couldn't. He had to prove himself.

"Then, after everyone is satisfied and your grandfather gets better, you'll go back home," the worker said. "Promise."

Edward was feeling much better now.

To be home, living with Grandpa, was what he wanted. But he still felt scared. What if it didn't happen? Now it was all up to him.

Then the worker left the room. Now he was alone with Mr. and Mrs. Lawrence. They both came over and each gave him a big hug.

He didn't want to be a poor sport, so he let them. Then he wiped his eyes with his fingers. He wasn't really crying, just clearing out his eyes.

"Instead of your foster son, can we just be pals?" he asked very quietly.

Mr. and Mrs. Lawrence nodded, their heads bobbing up and down like fishing floats.

"If you call us Joe and Ann," they said.

The boy chewed his lip and nodded back.

Chapter 2: A New Friend

It was different living in town instead of in the country. Edward told Grandpa everything that happened so far. "Getting used to a new family is tough. And I miss our little farm in Greenfield." He could only have short visits since Grandpa was very weak. "I'm trying really hard to be good."

"Edward. It's such a beautiful day," his foster mom said after they returned from the hospital. "You have to start spending time with your new friends."

He just shrugged.

"Maybe you could also go and pick up some milk," Ann said.

How could he tell her he felt like a wimp around new kids? It wasn't easy for a foster kid to make friends. He was even afraid of the dog next door.

His name was Ace, and he had a mean looking set of teeth. Edward watched Ace from his bedroom window this morning. He knew the dog heard him whisper, "Ace is waiting for me." Edward's heart pounded.

"Do I have to?" he asked Mrs. Lawrence. It was his job to walk to the store for milk. But right now?

"Yes!" Her voice was a command. "It's your job. We both agreed."

"B...but..." he stammered. No use. "What if I walk past

Ace and the dog eats me up—" Edward caught himself.
"Oops." Good thing she didn't hear him complaining. He
might have to go to bed a half hour early.

He had to watch himself in his new home. Edward
found out his foster dad could be quite a grouch if he
wasn't doing his chores.

Edward wore his fastest running shoes—new Nike
Speedsters—in case his feet had to zip away like Batman.

Ann gave him her usual mushy hug. But he didn't
mind, even though his face scrunched up. "Thanks,
Mom." The first time he called her Mom, she just looked
at him. Edward knew Ann liked it.

His eyes peeked around the corner. Ace was on the
sidewalk, chain clanking on the concrete. *Does he see me?*
Edward asked himself. Not yet. His new friends said Ace
was mean. Was he or not?

Edward's forehead was damp. His hands kept
squeezing each other, and his knees banged together.

He got down on his hands and knees and worked his
way around his own backyard then behind Ace's house.
So far so good, and now one more house to go then he'd
be home free.

His plan was working fine until Mrs. Lawrence yelled,
"Edward! Where are you?"

"Here." He tried to whisper. Now all his sneaking
around was ruined.

"You forgot the money. For the milk."

"Oh, no." Did Ace hear?

A bark. Then growls. Edward's feet did the Indy 500
back to the Lawrences' porch. Skidding to a stop, he
landed on top of Mrs. Lawrence's toes.

"Ouch," she said.

"Sorry."

"Then get off them."

He did.

"What's the matter?"

Could he lie to her? She looked like a fierce ninja warrior standing before him. Maybe she could protect him. So he told her.

"Oh, Edward! Come on, do you want to hold my hand?"

"No!"

"Well, what if I go first?"

"No. No." He had to face Ace. Even if his brave foster mom came along to protect him.

"Come on, let's go," she said. "You first."

What if he chickened out? What would his friends say?

They walked towards Ace. Then Edward's feet almost did a scared-cat dance. He looked back. Mrs. Lawrence was still coming. He had to go on. He had to be brave, for once in his life.

"Come on, Mom," he said meekly. "Stay close."

Ace walked slowly to the end of his chain. Then he stretched and yawned. His mouth looked like an alligator's, with lots of sharp teeth.

Edward stood still. He felt like an icicle.

Mrs. Lawrence said, "Pat him."

This was seriously bad news for Edward. He wanted to turn into a statue. His feet felt like cement blocks. His legs were like two tall towers. Electricity fizzled out of his head. "Don't move," he breathed.

Suddenly Ace came close. Edward thought the dog was at the end of his chain. But he wasn't. There was at least another couple of feet. Now he was sniffing Edward's legs and hands.

His foster mom was watching. She was smiling. Smiling? Why?

Mrs. Lawrence must know something he didn't. She didn't seem worried. Maybe the dog had rubber teeth.

Edward's hand touched Ace on the cheek. The dog's furry face was warm. And his nose felt like a wet sponge. Then Edward decided to be very brave. He crouched down and put his arm around the dog's neck.

This was really cool.

Ace looked up at him strangely.

Edward thought he was smiling.

Chapter 3: A Change in Plans

Grandpa couldn't come home. He needed special care. And the news was hard to understand for a young boy.

Edward went with his foster parents to the nursing home as often as he could.

He really missed having his Grandpa Jim walk with him.

The last couple visits all seemed the same. Grandpa just wasn't getting any better. Something must be wrong.

He had been so kind to Edward, having raised him for two years.

Now Edward wondered what would happen. Would the Lawrences keep him for a while longer?

It was something to think of.

Everyone in the nursing home looked so lonely. Edward wished he could take them all to his foster home. Especially Grandpa Jim.

Long corridors were lined with couches. Men and women sat and listened and watched everything going on. Some kept nodding their heads, trying hard to stay awake. Others tried to smile.

Would Grandpa forgive him for not being able to care for him? Edward looked around without staring. This visit, he would try hard not to be sad.

At home later that day, he asked, "Why does Grandpa still smile all the time? And he hardly talks anymore."

"Edward, your grandfather needs to be there," Mrs. Lawrence said. "That way, we know he's safe. Especially since he now needs a wheelchair."

The boy felt her words flow over him like gentle ocean waves. He knew his foster mother wanted to help him understand.

"I wish he was the way he always was," he answered. "I love him so much."

Edward's bedroom was full of creaks and groans tonight. He tried to imagine how hard it was for Grandpa. Like not being able to move around the way he used to.

Stars winked each time Edward blinked back tears. He clenched his hands and pretended he was right beside Grandpa.

Edward closed his eyes and remembered.

The first time he visited Grandpa in the nursing home was a shock. His wheelchair seemed so tiny. Edward knew Grandpa was sorry to be seen like that.

Grandpa used to take him to the stream back of the farm. He was there when Edward caught his first fish. It was an awesome seven-inch brook trout.

Now, Edward missed his encouraging words. Was Grandpa thinking of him right now?

Then there was the time when his foster mom and dad said Grandpa could hardly see anymore.

"Glaucoma" was a word that came like a robber.

"It took away his window to the world," his foster dad said.

When Edward visited after that, he had a hard time figuring why these things had to happen.

"It's part of life's plan," his foster dad said. "We don't understand, either, but on your next visit, I want you to watch your Grandpa's face. Don't speak, just watch."

Today, Edward did watch carefully. He saw Grandpa sitting in his wheelchair, parked tightly against the wall.

His face was raised upwards looking out the window. The sun bathed his face with brightness. Grandpa wore his usual broad smile. It was as if his wrinkled skin disappeared. A sound crept from his throat, dry and raspy at first.

His humming floated down the corridor. There were no words, just a soft melody. Grandpa seemed so content, sitting and staring out the window.

What did he see? Edward wondered.

He looked at his foster mom and foster dad. Would they be the same, some day? Would he be like them, too? Old and sickly, like Grandpa was right now? Would he have to sign them into a nursing home, too? Questions buzzed like mosquitoes around his head. They seemed so real, he almost swatted the air.

Edward was so busy thinking, he almost missed seeing the something special his foster parents said to watch for.

A robin jumped up on the ledge and was staring through the window. Its half opened beak seemed to be speaking. Then the robin's head tilted to one side as if it was listening to something.

Edward hardly breathed. He noticed his foster parents, their eyes wide with interest. His Grandpa was smiling and humming. He seemed to be singing to the robin.

It was really cool.

On the way home in the car, Edward tapped his foster dad on the shoulder. "Was that bird really listening to him? Did the robin actually hear his song?"

His foster parents didn't answer right away. Edward knew he had to be patient. They sometimes took a while to answer his questions.

It was all so mixed up. Maybe he had to work it out for himself.

"Your grandpa is like a young deer," his foster father finally said. "He's like a proud animal of the forest. That is why his face is covered in smiles."

Edward listened to every word.

"He also has such good memories," his foster mom said. "And you are a big part of them."

As Edward jumped into bed that night, he felt Grandpa's warmth. It was comfortable, like when he was a little boy sitting on Grandpa's lap. Now he turned his face to look through the window at the night sky.

He felt understanding sweep over him like an extra blanket. "Goodnight, Grandpa Jim. I miss having you home." The boy's voice seemed to float around the room.

Edward hummed a tune filled with good thoughts.

He vowed to continue hiking in the woods this summer, even if Grandpa was not able to. Like Grandpa, he would also pass on many smiles.

"Thank you, Grandpa Jim" sounded loud in his room as he fell asleep.

Chapter 4: The Angels Came

Edward remembered the phone call that came like a bolt of lightning. It woke everyone up. But Edward stayed in his room, somehow knowing it was bad news.

He was so upset, he could not even attend Grandpa's funeral yesterday.

Now words kept squirming up the stairs to his bedroom.

"It's so sad. Why doesn't he cry?"

"Yes, it must be hard on him," another voice said.

Edward got off his bed and lay on the floor. "I wonder if they can hear me?" he whispered to the dust balls.

The wooden floor scratched his nose as he listened.

"You know," the voice continued, "that young man without his grandfather..." Words became dark clouds. They were talking about him again.

He no longer wanted to hear those voices. They were like arrows that hurt. He sat on the floor and scrunched up his legs.

Downstairs, a lot of people were crying, including his foster parents, along with Grandpa's friends and neighbours, too. Edward bit his lip. He looked at the picture of himself and Grandpa on his dresser.

He looked around the room quickly. Then he got up

and walked around. His hands found a baseball. "Anyone want to play ball?" he asked, looking in the mirror.

Edward looked out his window. Several cars were parked in their driveway. He felt like an eagle perched on the second floor.

One day Grandpa had taken him out on the roof. "High as the sky," he had said. Good thing Grandpa had held on to Edward really tight. The boy had been fearful of heights.

"What if I fall?" he had asked then.

And his Grandpa had answered, "Then you'll have to learn how to fly like a pilot."

Grandpa knew that was Edward's dream.

His friend Ryan was downstairs in the yard. He might want to play ball with him.

Edward's feet changed like magic into a runaway car. He went roaring down the stairs. Like Superman, he flew across the kitchen. He was a thundering storm as he banged through the screen door.

Edward yelled out, "Ryan! Wanna play ball?"

And they did, friend with friend. Ryan kept looking at his chum. He had such a concerned face.

But it didn't bother Edward. He wanted to feel the smack of a ball into his glove. *Zap!* It didn't matter if his hands stung. It helped push away those unhappy feelings.

Ann called the boys in for lunch. "Really awesome. Grilled cheese sandwiches!" they said.

The Children's Aid worker pulled into the driveway. She gave Edward a special hug. She did the same for his friend Ryan, too.

Edward felt like a poor sport when he didn't give her

one back. "Why are your eyes so red?" he asked.

She didn't say anything. She just looked away.

The afternoon went by like a speeding train. Then Mrs. Lawrence made Edward a snack before bedtime.

When evening came, Edward heard the creaking on the stairs once more. And he became afraid. Was it Grandpa coming to say good night?

"No! No!" Edward's words were like spit. *Bad thoughts. Don't think of that.* A monster might come out of the closet and really torment him. Edward's eyes were bugged out.

And his heart beat faster, faster.

It was only Mrs. Lawrence. *Phew.* He was so concerned. Better not let her see he was almost beginning to bawl.

"Edward, I have something for you," Ann said. His foster mom was holding a brightly coloured package.

His pyjamas were warm and cozy. But chills began to run up and down his back.

His bed was so comfortable. But he watched his foster mom with sad eyes. His mind walked backwards in time, and he felt like a helpless little boy again. Like when he had to leave Grandpa to come here.

"It's a gift from your grandfather. He wanted to give it to you himself," she said. "Just before..." Her words were fuzzy.

Then his foster mom wrapped her arms around him. She was so cuddly. Just like his big teddy bear on the dresser. It helped take away some of his sad feelings.

Edward watched as she opened the box. "It's a bomber jacket," she said. "For a pilot." Then she put it beside him on the bed. "It was the one he used to wear."

Edward saw tears on her cheeks as she bent to kiss him on the forehead.

Once she left, he lay on the bed and watched the jacket as if it would start flying around the room by itself. It was brown with badges on the arms.

Edward thought about his grandpa. He wished with all his heart he was right here beside him. He could almost hear Grandpa's laughter in his ears. His silly jokes were so funny.

"Ha. Ha. Ha," sounds escaped Edward's lips. Just the way Grandpa used to do it.

Edward could not cry. He would not believe his grandpa died in the nursing home. The man he loved so much must be somewhere else.

Suddenly his feet had a mind of their own. He jumped out of bed and padded over to the window.

The moon had a large smile. It was as if the man-in-the-moon were calling to him. "Oh, Eddie," it seemed to say. "Have I got a surprise for you."

Edward picked up the bomber jacket...Grandpa's special gift. He put it on and zipped it up. The leather smelled like oil and grease, and he imagined it fit just right.

He opened the window, his fingers finding strength he didn't think possible.

Now he was on the windowsill. His hair no longer flapped in the wind. A leather helmet covered his head.

Outside his window, a plane was waiting just for him. He looked down and saw he was wearing fine boots and pants.

He stepped into his plane. And the propellers began to turn slowly then faster.

Edward sat back and studied the instruments. He pulled a switch, and the plane took off.

It flew across town and high above the buildings. The plane turned and twisted in the inky space.

As the plane climbed towards the stars, he felt a thrill. Edward was flying all by himself. He began his journey to look for Grandpa. *He's out there somewhere. He has to be.*

Is he behind the clouds? Edward flew and checked. *Or is he hiding over that mountain?* He checked that out, too.

What about that island? Edward flew low over the waves. He could not see a thing.

Edward looked everywhere. Where was his grandpa?

Then tired eyes began to close, and Edward turned towards home. It was as if a bell sounded in the back of his head.

"Time to go home," it seemed to say. His comfortable bed was waiting.

He parked his plane and stepped into his room. When he looked back, the plane was gone.

Edward put his boots and pants on the bed. Soon, they disappeared, too. He took off his leather helmet and put it beside his pillow. And he lay down, wearing his bomber jacket gift.

Then Edward fell asleep, still dreaming of his grandpa. His tired head was full of sounds. Airplane noises and wind made him feel like a log drifting on the ocean.

He saw faces. Ann and Joe and Grandpa Jim. All were smiling.

When Edward woke up the next morning, it was sunny. His mom was calling. Edward dressed and went downstairs. He was still wearing his bomber jacket.

Breakfast was bacon and one egg. And juice. There

was even a glass of milk. "To build bones," he said before Ann did.

"It's time," his foster mom said. Now Edward's tummy felt tight. "We have to sort out some things," she added gently.

He knew she was right. Somehow, the hurt had to come out.

He remembered last night. About flying toward the stars. He knew now why he could not find his grandpa.

He closed his eyes and saw that smiling face again. This time it said, "Ha. Ha. Ha. Couldn't find me last night, eh?"

Edward went with his foster mom to the cemetery.

It was a sad walk, because Edward came to say goodbye.

Standing in front of Grandpa Jim's grave, Edward finally cried.

Chapter 5: Time to Forgive

Edward knew he would never forget Grandpa. The kids at school couldn't really understand. Coming from his little family of two to a foster home was not easy.

He didn't know things would get even tougher.

On one school day, sadness crept down the street. It came as a shadow with sharp teeth. When the words were spoken, they were dark and mean.

"You're just a foster kid!" rang sharp like a knife. It was cruel. And to Edward, it felt like a hot blade going through butter.

Instead, the words were going through him. He was like the butter. It wasn't his fault he didn't have a family anymore. Why did Grandpa Jim have to die, anyway?

The day began with his usual activities. Get out of bed, hurry up and get dressed. Then wash his face and tear downstairs.

Edward could smell the coffee. But he wasn't supposed to have any. It was for his "grouchy" foster dad. Freckles on his face wrinkled up. One day, the teacher read to the class that caffeine was in coffee. "Not good for children," she said.

Being a foster kid was not such fun either, he thought.

"Hi, Mom! Hi, Mr. Lawrence!"

"Not so loud," his foster mom said.

"SSSH," Mr. Lawrence said. "How come you don't call me Dad?"

Edward didn't feel like saying anything more. His leg was sore today. He hurt it playing soccer yesterday after school. Sitting down, he quietly ate breakfast.

"I like Mom better," he mumbled under his breath.

Three mouths were like vacuum cleaners. All the food was munched. Then everyone got into Mom's car. And then he was off to school.

Edward liked being in Miss Morrison's class. She was always kind. Maybe she felt sorry for him, because of his grandfather.

But today, he came into his class like a scared deer. He knew the class bully was waiting. His words stung like a bee, again and again.

"Foster kid, foster kid" became loud whispers behind his back. They crawled like spiders under his arms. Edward somehow knew today was going to be different. He felt it in his bones. The feeling went right down to his toes.

His love for Grandpa would always keep him strong.

Edward opened up his book and read, "There once was a little boy. He was a foster child. Some people made fun of him."

It can't be, he thought. *It sounds just like me.* "And the boy had lots of freckles," the story said on the next page.

He quickly read the words over again. "Awesome," he said. His own face was full of freckles.

"What's that?" Miss Morrison asked. "Did you say something, Edward?"

"No, Miss," he answered. "N...N...Nothing."

"All right, everyone. Start reading your story on page forty-one in your *Living Reader*."

Then the teacher sent another chill down his back. "It's called 'A Day at Summer Camp.'"

Edward looked around. His story on the same page was different, even though his book had the same cover as the others. He borrowed Ryan's for a moment. It had the same number of pages.

But his was a different story. It was called "The Bully." Should he say anything?

He didn't.

Then he read more. His eyes grew wide as he read the part about two wishes for the foster boy. Then the bell rang for lunch.

"Shucks." He wanted to see what happened next.

Imagine that. The foster boy in the story could have any two wishes. *I wonder if I can, too?*

At the school cafeteria, everyone pushed and shoved. His elbow got bumped. And his hot dog bounced off his plate.

The class bully stood there with a mean look on his face. Then he stepped on Edward's lunch. Ketchup and mustard squirted through the air and landed on Edward's clean shirt.

He didn't dare say anything. He bit his lower lip. The bully had a sneer on his face. He looked like a cat that just captured a mouse.

Edward had a hard time keeping tears from crawling down his cheeks. When you had no parents and no grandpa, it was hard to be brave.

Everybody's picking on me, he thought. He left the cafeteria and snuck outside. Now his leg felt really sore.

Edward didn't notice the bully following along with two of his friends.

"Hey, you," the bully said.

"Yah. We got to talk to you," one of his chums added.

And Edward shivered. He wasn't cold. There wasn't any wind. It was fear. It was like a dark blanket covering him.

The bully placed his face right in front of Edward's. "Foster kid, foster kid," came from his wide mouth.

Finally, Edward could take it no longer. "I wish you had a real sore leg, too," he said. And it happened, quick as a seagull swallowing a fish.

The bully yelled out. "OW! OW! My leg!"

He started to move away from Edward. And his leg dragged along with him. Edward just stared. His wish really happened. Just like in the book.

The bully and his friends left quickly. They seemed to be afraid of Edward. They forgot all about eating their lunches.

Edward could hardly believe his eyes. They were afraid of him? He became brave and followed the bully right to his house.

The bully's mother came out, seeing her boy on the front steps. "What happened?" she asked, looking at Edward.

"He called me names."

"Names?"

"Like foster kid."

"David, that's not fair. Why did you say those things?" She was quite upset with her son.

David put his head down.

Edward walked over to the tree in front of David's

house. He listened to the bully crying. David's mother was still hollering at him.

Crows were calling *caw caw* at Edward. *Maybe they want me to forgive David,* he thought. One landed on the sidewalk. It looked at him.

Edward decided to correct the situation. He scratched his chin and made a second wish.

Suddenly, there was a very loud and happy "YAHOO!" from David. "Mommm! My leg feels much better now!"

And Edward knew things were going to be much better at school, too. He couldn't wait to get home.

What a story he had to tell at supper.

Chapter 6: At the Beach

Today was a special treat day, for just Edward and his mom. The tide was in. Salty water licked at the shore. Patches of froth splashed the beach.

Edward loved the ocean. He could sit and watch it for hours. "Mom! Mom!"

Mrs. Lawrence looked up. "What?"

"Did ya see the boat? Watch me skip a rock? Can I go for a swim?" Edward spoke more confidently now. His sore leg was better, and he had no further problems at school.

Joe was working some more overtime and couldn't make it today.

"Can I, Mom? Huh?" Edward was full of his usual questions.

"Which answer do you want?" Ann Lawrence asked.

"Just say yes."

"Yes."

"Thanks, Mom." Edward skipped a rock. It went *KERPLUNK.*

"Shucks," he said.

"Is it okay if I lie back now?"

"No, not yet. Come on. Watch me, Mom."

"Well, okay. How many skips are you going to do?"

KERPLUNK. His rock didn't skip. It just went

KERPLUNK. Edward wanted his mom to see how well he could do.

He was the best rock skipper at Big Cove beach. He proved it last weekend when he did ten skips. Even his new buddies said he was awesome.

The sun was hot, and, thankfully, Ann had her UV protection on.

Many children came to Big Cove beach to swim. Some, like themselves, came from as far away as Truro to lie on the beach.

Others came from New Glasgow and nearby Merigomish. *Oh-my-gosh Merigomish.* Edward thought that was funny.

He said it out loud this time. "Oh-my-gosh, Merigomish." The words were like a poem.

"What's that?" Ann called out.

"Nothing," he answered.

Edward began to look for a perfect rock. It had to be small, like a quarter. Edward yelled out, "May I just go over to that big tree?"

Ann stood up and said, "No farther than that."

His feet were cooking on the warm sand. His toes felt like sausages on a hot stove. But the wind was cool. It sort of tickled his back. Waves crashed and slapped upon the beach.

Stepping on mushy seaweed was gross on his feet. But it took the burning away.

Edward did not like to touch dried up crab shells. Instead, he picked up coloured bits of clam shells. He searched for nice rounded rocks and tried several to see how they fit his hand.

The first one felt funny. It had a big lump on the side,

and he was able to get a good grip. Standing sideways, he faced the ocean, feet spread out. Toes dug into the sand until they were almost hidden.

"Take that, you!" he shouted. He was a sailor ready to set sail. His rock was going to be his speedboat. It would ride the waves. It would skip over and over. It would even hit the other side—he hoped.

His arm reached way back. Then he quickly bent forward and threw with all his might. As Edward's fingers let go, the rock flew like a rocket towards the water. *KERPLUNK!*

The ocean quickly swallowed it. A lazy seagull seemed to be smiling at him. "Not fair!" he shouted.

The joke was on him. He could only do two skips today. Not ten like before. If only he could be a seal. Maybe under the water was a perfect stone just waiting for him.

He walked back and forth along the beach until he was tired.

"Mom, let's you and me do something." He soon forgot about rock skipping.

Edward and his foster mom played in the sand. Their contest was to build the best sandcastle.

Ann won.

They had a tickling contest.

She won again.

"Mom? I bet I could beat you at skipping rocks."

"You think so?" she teased. "Are you rested enough? After all, I was the winner in the last two contests."

"Yes, yes. I am." He smiled back at her.

The bet was on. It would be his chance to show her. Edward would be the best rock-skipping champion in all of Nova Scotia.

It would be fun to beat his foster mom at something.

He searched the beach and under bits of wood that drifted ashore. Edward even checked around the seaweed. "No. Nothing there," he said.

Then he found the perfect rock. It was flat like a soda cracker, the same size as a Toonie. It felt like a winner. He knew he would finally win the contest this time.

Edward practiced how he would laugh after he won. Just like Grandpa used to laugh. "Ha! Ha! Ha!" or just "Ha. Ha." Maybe "I beat you" or "I won. I won."

If Joe could be right here, he'd say, "Edward! Please stop that bragging."

Edward wished he could be his foster parents' very own son. Sometimes he pretended he was. Edward wondered what his foster dad would say about that.

Maybe he shouldn't laugh out loud. It might upset Ann. Edward thought of the many times his foster mom helped him.

Mrs. Lawrence was beside him whenever he cried over a problem. She caught his balloon one day when it escaped. Today, she even lifted him out of the ocean when he swallowed a mouthful of salt water. And she didn't even laugh. Well, not too hard, anyways.

And yesterday, those hot dogs were so tasty. His foster mother also gave him the best hugs any boy could want. He didn't mind them so much now.

Would it be fair to beat her at rock skipping? Maybe he should think about something else to do.

"Edward?"

"Yeah, Mom?"

"What are you doing?"

"I'm thinking," he said. He put his winning rock in the pocket of his short pants.

"Come here and see what I found," Ann said.

He went over and patiently waited. She had a nice round rock. It looked almost as good as the one he had.

Edward knew he had the one to win any contest. But it didn't seem so important now. He looked thoughtfully at her and said, "I know another game we could play."

"Is it a new game?" Ann asked.

"Yes."

"Is it a fun game?"

"Yes."

"Do you think you can beat me?"

"Yes, yes," he yelled.

"Okay, what is it?"

"The first one to say 'I LOVE YOU' ten times!" he shouted.

Edward won. And his smile was a mile wide.

Chapter 7: Time to Dream

The sun was dropping hot rays on their little town of Truro. Edward stared across the street at the woods in Victoria Park.

Ann looked angry as she came around the corner of the house.

"Edward? Are you daydreaming again? Don't you have chores?"

He closed his eyes to both questions. She was looking after him for now. But would it always be this way?

How much longer would he live here? Soon, he would be all grown up and living on his own. He hoped he wouldn't grow up too quickly.

"Yes," he whispered. "And my chores are finished."

"Joe will be glad to hear the chores are done."

"I was just thinking about all them trees," Edward said.

"What do you want to be this time?"

"I was thinking about being a lumberjack."

"Why?"

"I can chop them down."

"Why?"

"Then I could build a bigger room for each of us."

"Almost nine years old and thinking of things like that." She sighed. "I know your room is tiny. But one day we'll get another house. You'll see."

When she left, he sat down on the front lawn.

"I wanna be a carpenter," he said out loud. "Then I can make everything just the way I want it." *I can measure good, too,* he thought.

At the school science fair last month, his model of a town was really neat. "I will be a carpenter, and I'll be the best there is, too."

"BREAKFAST!" rang across the yard. His foster father's voice was louder than any dinner bell.

Edward quickly joined Ann and Joe at the kitchen table.

"Okay...eat." In the kitchen, Ann was the boss. Cereal, toast, and juice disappeared into mouths. They finished up everything.

That afternoon, everyone went to the outdoor pool. Edward felt the water cover his toes. He watched other kids yelling and screaming. They looked happy. He wished he could just scream and yell like them.

"I wanna be a lifeguard," he said aloud. "Then maybe I could sit high on a lookout, too. I'll take training for swimming and learn everything I can. Then I'll be ready if someone needs help."

"Edward! What are you doing?" His foster father was being a grouch again. "Stop daydreaming! Get in the water, or we'll go home right now!"

Then Edward was swimming and splashing like the rest of the kids.

It seemed to make them happy. He just wanted everyone to be happy. He knew they were really kind. Not just strict. When his grandfather died, it was hard.

"Don't worry all the time," his foster mom said.

"You're just a little boy. Things have a way of working out."

He was glad he had a place to live.

"I wish I was a doctor and worked in the hospital," he told Ann. "Then I can help everyone who's sick."

The evening sky looked like it was painted with red and yellow colours. Edward felt very tired.

It had been a long, long day.

He hurried to the supper table. Tonight's treat was fish and chips. *Yummy!*

Mr. Lawrence was grouchy again. Mrs. Lawrence was smiley and quiet, as usual.

And Edward was his usual serious self, biting his lips and showing worried looks. He tried so hard today.

His daydreaming and imagination helped him along. Maybe he should stop wishing so much. He just wanted everything to be A-okay.

He wanted these folks to really like him.

Ready for bed meant getting pyjamas on and brushing teeth. Suddenly, from his bedroom window, Edward saw a shooting star. The streaking light became a *KABOOM* and lit up the sky.

It really caught his attention and took away his sad thoughts. "I wish I was an astronaut." His mind raced excitedly. "Then I could leap-frog over the stars. Just like Captain Picard on TV."

Suddenly, he knew it was time to be brave again. The last time was when he visited Grandpa's grave for the first time.

Edward put away his wishing imagination, at least for now. Maybe it was the *KABOOM* in the sky that got him full of energy.

He giggled to himself as he thought about what he was going to do. Edward rushed into the next room and smacked each of his foster parents with his pillow.

His laughter followed him as he ran from one side of the bed to the other.

"What is it? What's wrong?" Ann and Joe asked in alarm. They looked in wonder at this active little boy.

"I just want to give you a goodnight hug and a big fat kiss!" Edward said with a great big smile. They stared at their foster son with huge eyes as he jumped onto the bed.

Edward gave his nice mom and grouchy foster dad a great big squishy hug. And his kisses on their cheeks were really squishy. "I wish you would adopt me. Right now!" he shouted.

Then he ran back to his room, before their shock wore off.

Tomorrow was fishing time.

And summer was sure to be fun.

Chapter 8: More Fishing

Pesky deer flies munched on Edward. His face and hands were covered with spotted black wings. Wasn't fishing supposed to be fun?

"Mr. Lawrence!" he shouted. "I need more bug spray!"

His foster father came beside him and sprayed his hands. And rubbed some on his neck. Then his shirt and pants received a spray for extra protection.

"Stop calling me Mister. It's Joe, okay?"

"Yup." It would be different, but Edward would try. He was happy to go fishing today. He really felt good since the words he said last night jumped from his mouth.

To be adopted. Now that would be something.

It was early June, and it rained a lot lately. That meant an army of bugs. Big time. Edward wore rubber boots, long pants, and a long sleeved shirt.

He was hot and sweaty, but he was having fun.

"Hey! I got a bite!" he yelled at the trees. His voice carried across the creek and through the valley, as an echo.

Edward lifted his fishing rod just like Mr. Lawrence said. The brook trout swung towards him and landed with a plop on the grass.

Then it jumped around a bit.

Mr. Lawrence held it firmly. Edward couldn't stand

the touch of the slimy body. His blue eyes were like trapeze flyers. Up and down. Up and down with excitement.

"My first fish...Joe," he said quietly after his arm waving stopped. Good thing his friends didn't see how he acted.

"I'm proud of you, Edward," Mr. Lawrence said. "I'll just be over there. See if you can catch another." Then he disappeared behind a few trees and a forest of ferns.

"Now I'm all by myself," Edward said. "And the fish in this spot are mine." His voice travelled once again through the valley. "ALL MINE...ALL MINE."

Edward pushed his worm closer to the end of the hook. Just like Mr. Lawrence...Joe showed him. Then he placed his thumb on the control of the fishing reel. He swung his arm towards the pool of water. Just as Edward finished his swing, he lifted his thumb. "Wowie!" he said as the spinner with the worm splashed into the water.

"Why are you throwing that into the water?"

Edward turned suddenly and saw a boy dressed in funny clothes. "Who are you?"

"I'm Nathan," the stranger answered.

"You look just like a pirate," Edward said.

"I am a pirate."

"You are?"

"Our ship is over there beyond the marsh." The pirate boy pointed off across the pool of water. "What manner of clothing is that? Your head covering is also strange."

"You mean my cap?" Edward asked. He stared bug-eyed at the stranger, who looked to be about twelve years old. "You're a pirate?"

"Aye. I am that." The boy pounded his chest.

"You won't hurt me, will ya?" Edward asked.

"Not a little tyke like thee," the boy said. "Ta. Ta. I must be off." Then he was gone.

Edward sat down on the ground and shook his head. *Maybe it was the heat,* he thought. *I chickened out before that kid.* When he heard a rustling in the bush, Edward jumped up quickly.

It was Mr. Lawrence, not the boy again.

"Any more luck?"

"Nope," Edward answered. Should he tell about the boy he was talking to? No, maybe not.

At school, everybody said Edward made up stories. "Oh no, not that 'wishing' boy again."

Would Mr. Lawrence believe him?

"Guess what..." Edward began.

Mr. Lawrence came over and sat down beside him. "Okay. What's up? You look so serious."

Edward told him about Nathan. He was so talky he didn't even notice the deer flies or the mosquitoes. But he did see the questions on Mr. Lawrence's face.

He knew Mr. Lawrence didn't believe him. He watched his foster father get up.

"You're making this up."

"No, I'm not."

"I think you are."

"No!"

"Edward, don't be silly."

The boy was so upset, he flung a branch into the pool of water.

"You'll scare the fish," Mr. Lawrence said.

"I don't care."

"You don't, do you?"

"No!"

"Then it's time to go home. Let's go." Mr. Lawrence picked up his fishing pole and started through the woods.

Edward ran after him. His eyes had tear spots. "Why don't you believe me?"

Mr. Lawrence stopped then turned and looked at Edward. It was very hot. The bugs were also very pesky.

And Edward hadn't even complained one little bit.

"I'm only a kid, Mr. Lawrence. You have to be patient with me."

"It's Joe," Mr. Lawrence reminded him. He watched Edward carefully. "Edward?"

"Yes."

"I really think you are brave. After leaving you alone by yourself."

"Thanks, Joe. And I'm really glad you took me fishing. I'm not used to these woods. It's a little scary."

"Do you want to go home now?"

"No." Edward's voice was almost a whisper. His head hung low.

Mr. Lawrence placed his hand under Edward's chin and lifted it.

Edward's eyes were blue, like the sky. They were also clear like fresh water. He was covered with bug bites all over his forehead and neck. And his blond hair was all messed up.

"You like to read a lot, don't you?"

"Yes, a lot."

"Do you like stories about pirates?"

Edward answered, "Yes, I do."

Then Mr. Lawrence said, "Edward, I believe you. Only next time, call me. I'd like to meet this pirate friend of yours."

The boy's cheeks were pinched, because his smile was so large. *The grouch believes me,* Edward thought. *Someone finally believes me.*

Mr. Lawrence headed for the waiting pool of water. He looked back and said, "Let's get back to fishing."

Edward didn't need to be asked a second time.

"Wait 'til Mom hears about this trip!" he yelled out.

Chapter 9: Oh-Oh, I Forgot

Edward sat on the front porch waiting for his mom. She should be there by now. He was upset from waiting so long.

His Sunday school teacher always said, "Count to ten."

Could he help it if he had a temper tantrum once in a while? "Mom, where are you?"

He could imagine his foster mom at work, not even worrying about him. *She's probably at her computer desk right now, typing away.*

Probably chewing gum, too, he thought. "I wish I had a piece of Double Bubble."

Edward looked down at his black and white TNT Joggers. Joe said they were "nifty." He usually worked through lunch, so Edward couldn't get angry with him today.

But Mom was always there at noon, on time. He just had to wait. *Hey! Maybe I'll stay home this afternoon,* he thought.

A little voice inside said, *Be patient.*

"YIPES. Almost 12:30," he said, glancing at his watch. "I have to be at the Truro Boys and Girls Club by 1:00 P.M." Edward felt weak from hunger.

He must have worn himself out playing at Ryan's house before coming home.

By the time Ann came, he'd probably be just a pile of bones. The front step would be all cluttered up with them.

What if he left now? His tummy said to wait. His legs said to go.

Just then, Joe showed up. *Will he believe I sat here for almost my whole lunch time? And I almost starved to death.* Edward wanted to say something nasty. But then he would be just like the grouch.

"What are you doing sitting there?"

Edward told him. He put on his saddest voice. He wanted Joe to feel sorry for him.

"My tummy was shrinking. And the skin would soon be falling off these bones. Soon the wind will come along and blow me away."

His foster dad's eyes got really huge. "Eddie." Usually "Eddie" meant he was going to say something really grouchy. But he closed his mouth then opened it again. Finally, he said, "You silly goose, Edward."

"Don't call me names," Edward yelled back.

"You forgot. Oh Edward, you forgot!" Then his foster dad started laughing. It made Edward confused. Joe wasn't usually in a laughing mood.

"It's not funny! I'm hungry! Mom's not here! She doesn't even care about me!" Edward was on the verge of tears.

Joe came close and looked him in the eye. "Edward," he said softly. "Mom did make your lunch. You forgot she had to work through lunch today. I just came home to get my briefcase."

Edward jumped back in horror. He did forget. "OMIGOSH!" was all he could say. "Oh no." His lunch was in Ryan's fridge.

"OMIGOSH. I forgive her. I forgive her." What was wrong with him?

He had even helped his mom last night.

Peanut butter and banana sandwiches and cookies and an apple, and...he better get going. She even gave him his favourite drink, chocolate milk.

"For a special treat, because I won't be here," Ann had said.

How could he think such mean things about her? "Tell...Mom...I'm...sorry!" he shouted.

Edward looked at his watch. He still had twenty minutes to eat his lunch at Ryan's then get to the Boys and Girls Club.

"GOTTA GO!" Edward yelled.

Joe yelled, "Be careful! Watch out for cars!"

But Edward had already taken off.

His feet were like thunder as they pounded on the pavement. *Go! Go! Go!* His feet hollered.

And he made it in time for the next program of activities.

Chapter 10: A Holiday

Edward and his foster parents decided to go for a few days' visit to check on Grandpa Jim's cottage. The Last Will and Testament said it now belonged to his grandson, Edward.

It was to be his, forever.

But Edward wished Grandpa got over his illness instead.

He sat on the edge of a hill, watching the lobster boats. It was the middle of August. Summer was flying by, and he was getting restless.

He liked getting up early in the morning by himself. His foster mom and dad were still sleeping.

Edward counted seven boats crossing back and forth. They were laying their lobster traps.

Grandpa kept one as a souvenir beside his summer cottage. It was shaped like a barrel cut in half, with netting down one end and a hole in the centre, called a head.

Northumberland Strait was mostly smooth, though small waves did reach the shore. Just behind it was Prince Edward Island, like a huge rock in the Atlantic Ocean.

Before Grandpa died two months ago, he and Edward

launched a mason jar. It used to have relish in it, but that day it held a note.

Grandpa Jim understood this was a lonely place for a little boy.

The note in the bottle said it all:

*Hi. I'm EDWARD LAPOINTE. I'm almost
ten years old. WANT to be my FRIEND?
I like to SWIM and play NINTENDO. I live
at – Lapointe's Cottage #4. GENERAL
DELIVERY, CAP LUMIERE, NB.*

Grandpa didn't think Edward's bottle idea was silly at all. When the jar floated away on an ocean swell, Edward wished it would bring back a friend!

He hoped something exciting would happen soon. Like someone finding his bottle. Wouldn't that be awesome?

He wondered if Ann liked it here at Grandpa Jim's place. Well, at least it used to be.

It was not so bad here by the ocean shore. The house had a lot of windows. And he was able to see every sunrise and sunset. This morning, he could almost feel the pink and red colours on his face.

There was even a natural rock stairway into the salt water from the shore. In some places, the water was very deep. Edward was careful to stay in the protected section where there was a little sandy beach.

After a short swim, he lay on his stomach and watched the ocean. He kept his eyes on the whitecaps. Edward wished they would bring a message from someone in England.

Or even France, where his great, great grandfather was born.

His eyes followed the sun climbing the sky. His chest felt the cool earth begin to warm up.

Ann called, "Time for lunch."

Then she asked, "Want to go for a ride after? It's a good day for a drive, and I'll show you some beautiful white-sand beaches."

"Yes," Joe agreed. "It will take your mind off that bottle. At least for a while."

"Don't worry," Ann said. "Your bottle will be found. Someday."

"You really think someone will find it and write to me?"

"Yes."

"Okay then," Edward said.

Joe stayed behind to continue painting the cottage.

And Edward and his foster mom began their trip to Buctouche, half an hour away. He enjoyed travelling along the seashore. As they arrived in the Acadian fishing village, he shouted, "Ya, look! The beach is white!"

"This is also the oyster-bed capital of New Brunswick," Ann said.

After visiting some souvenir shops and the bakery, Edward became restless and wanted to go home. He was tired of sightseeing. He had to get back to his lookout by the sea.

What if his bottle was found and someone was trying to get him?

Just then, Ann's cell phone rang. As she spoke, a smile came across her face. Edward wondered what was going on. "Okay, we'll be right there," she said.

Their car wheels carried them swiftly back home.

As soon as they stopped at the house, Joe yelled. "Edward! Quickly! A telephone call came for you awhile ago."

Shouting turned to a whisper when his foster dad leaned closer and said, "Someone found your bottle."

Edward's eyes bugged out. "My bottle? Someone found it?" His lips felt frozen. More words could hardly sneak out. "So you talked with..."

"Yes...phone. Quickly."

"Who?" Edward asked. He didn't understand at first. It was so unexpected.

"A boy walking on the shore a few miles away found your bottle last week," Joe said.

"He found it here?" Edward asked, disappointment showing on his face. "Not England or France?" He was hoping someone from really far away would find it.

"Just phone," Ann said.

And he did just that. "My name is Edward Lapointe," he said slowly and carefully. And his new friend's name was Jacques Forget. Both boys had a great time getting to know each other on the phone.

Their chatter moved noisily from one home to another. Jacques explained he was so excited to find the note. He spoke good English, and—guess what?—he wanted a new friend, too. And Edward became that friend.

The next day, Edward and Jacques went swimming at Grandpa's shore. Even though it was Edward's now, in his heart it would always be Grandpa's.

Imagine finding someone your own age just a few miles away at Richibucto Village. Edward shook his head in amazement.

He spent the afternoon with his new friend. But soon it was time for Edward and his foster parents to leave. Addresses were exchanged and promises made to write each other.

That is, until the next time they met.

Tomorrow was very special. Ann and Joe were taking Edward to a family reunion in New Brunswick. And they had to leave early in the morning.

The Lawrences could hardly wait for Edward to meet their relatives.

Chapter 11: Family Reunion

At first, it was exciting heading along the shore road. Places like Pointe de Bute, Port Elgin and Upper Cape were tiny villages.

Then setting up their trailer and eating with a whole army of children and adults was fun. But Edward was getting restless. He already missed his pal Jacques.

Edward tossed stones as he sat on the ocean shore. And waited impatiently for his foster parents' nephews and niece.

"Are they coming or not?" he said out loud. This hike was his idea. Usually, people didn't listen to his suggestions.

Today, they did.

But he wished they would hurry up. His sandy hair flopped loosely over his ears. He flung another flat stone. This one made three skips. The next one went *KERPLUNK!*

He kicked at the sand. Nearby, the smash and splash of heavy waves were loud on Northumberland Strait's shore. "Come on, hurry up," he muttered to himself.

"Finally!" he yelled out, as a single file of walkers came into view.

Led by his foster dad Joe, others hurried along. Then Troy ran ahead, trying to be first in line. Peter and his sister Joan were followed by another cousin, William. He was going to Dalhousie University in Halifax.

"All right, everybody," Joe called out. "Let's take our time and see what we can find on the shore."

This is so much fun, Edward thought.

The family reunion was held at Cape Spear, near Port Elgin, New Brunswick.

"Relatives are here from all over Nova Scotia and New Brunswick," Ann had told him earlier.

Joe had said, "I think it's a good idea for you to meet our relatives."

At the time, Edward wasn't sure why, but, if it made them happy, why not?

A little thought had circled inside his head. "No, it can't be," he had scolded himself. They had never mentioned his request to be adopted. "So, I just better be good," he had decided.

Now Edward wanted this hike as an escape from all the hugs and kisses. It also helped take away the pain of not having Grandpa Jim here with him.

He kept wishing with all his heart to be a part of some family. Forever. Not just be a foster son. Nor even just a pal.

The sky was painted a dull blue, and the wind blew noisily across the beach. It kept the group walking in a huddle, conversations all going at once.

Joan was the smallest in the group. "Mr. Lawrence, would you carry my sandals?" She was seven years old and not shy at all. Edward didn't like the way she always tried to take over. Since he was new here, he felt he should get a little extra attention. And he resented her competition.

At school, no one really noticed him. But here, well, it was his turn. Since Grandpa died, he was hoping for some extra sympathy.

"The magic word?"

"Please," she said to Mr. Lawrence, eyes rolling.

"All right, Joan. I'll carry them for you."

"Oh, girls," Edward huffed. He squinted in her direction as the sun shone on his well tanned features. He puckered his brow in annoyance.

The shoreline received a thorough going-over from the children. Nothing was missed.

"What treasures," Edward stammered. His eager rush took him to something broken, with a rope attached. "What is it?" When he was involved in a new adventure, he didn't want to miss a thing.

William knew this "find" and said, "It's a bobber, once used with a lobster trap. It floats and marks the fisherman's spot."

"You must be really smart," Edward said, trying to butter up William.

"He should know," young Joan piped up. "After all, he lived most of his life on the Cape Spear shore."

"Look at that!" Edward shouted, changing the subject.

He raced to a bright green object embedded in the sand. They chased after Edward.

"That's just a chunk of glass, no good for nothin'," Troy bellowed. He was quite disappointed it wasn't a cannon ball or something ancient.

"Come on, Troy," Joe said patiently to his nephew. "Take a good look at what Edward spotted. You might learn something."

They carefully examined the slender green and white

square chunk. The edges were smoothed out as if someone filed them down.

Edward finally felt special as everyone checked out his newly discovered treasure. This was his moment of glory. It was also cool how his foster dad made him feel important. Edward loved it.

"It's caused by friction," Joe continued. "Think of all the travelling and tumbling this piece did. Turning over and over, pushed back and forth by the rolling force of many waves. And for thousands of years."

Peter said, "Let's go in for a dip." On a very warm day with white sand underfoot, the suggestion made sense.

"Great! Come on! YAYYY!" Everyone pulled off running shoes and T-shirts. Joan and Edward already had their bathing suits on and were first in the water. Splashing each other seemed to start a shrieking and shouting contest.

"YIPES! C-c-cold!" they shouted together.

The rest of the group stopped suddenly and thought about the swim again. Maybe it wasn't such a good idea. Joe tried to coax them back into the water.

"No way...much too cold." In a moment, everyone agreed.

Someone hollered for a story, and, after some coaxing, Joe told one.

"A boy and girl were lost on the beach," Joe said. "Then they found a fisherman's deserted house..." He paused, noticing everyone listening "...and hearing *rap rap*, they went in.

"The mysterious sound led them upstairs and into each bedroom. Finally, they stood before an old dresser..." Joe stopped and looked around. Everyone was listening.

"They opened each drawer until finally there was only one left—the one the sound of *rap rap* came from. And they opened the drawer slowly, ever so slowly, and they found...WRAPPING PAPER!"

Everyone screamed and fell off the large driftwood log. Then they began laughing and poking one another.

Edward had fun listening and sitting by the ocean. "That story was better than eating a whole bag of chips," he said. Then he closed his eyes and wished he had lots of relatives like this.

It would be nice to be related to these kids. Then he could really be part of a family reunion.

The tide continued moving out, leaving shallow pools behind. Everyone made slapping sounds with bare feet on the remaining water.

William dipped his hand in the water and showed everyone a handful of crill. "These are tiny shrimp that whales eat in huge gulps," he said. His hand was full of scooting movements.

The crill looked like tiny pink spiders.

Large bar clams dotted the beach. And smaller sea clams were scattered about, too. They were now left high and dry after their journey into shore with the waves.

"More natural treasures for us," Edward said proudly.

He looked in wonder at dark coloured mussels. They were joined together in piggy-back bunches, hidden among the water-drenched foliage.

No matter where he searched, something unique made itself known.

Edward's eyes were large with each new discovery.

The ocean was calm as the afternoon came to a close.

Just as the group neared the main campground, adult voices called loudly, "Troy! Peter! Joan! Edward! Supper!"

The children raced off with answering calls of, "We're coming!"

William and Joe stood together for a brief moment as they watched the children.

"Joe! William! Race you back!" Edward shouted as his feet ploughed through the sand.

They were like children once again as they took up the challenge.

And the wiener-roast campfire that night was even more fun.

Chapter 12: More Adventures

It was so hot, trying to sleep last night. But the campfire and singsongs were fun. Getting up early this morning to fish was a real challenge, and it was still only ten o'clock.

Edward jumped out of the car, slamming the door. "Thanks, William, for taking me!"

"Mom! Joe!" he shouted at the trailer parked on the edge of the campground. He could see sleepy faces anxiously peering out.

Edward held onto the fishing creel slung over his shoulder. It held five speckled trout. "Mom! Joe!" His eyes were dancing. He could still feel the tugs the fish gave back in the brook.

His feet went *Thud! Thud!* up two steps.

Joan met him at the door. "Did you catch lots of big fish?"

"Yes! Yes!" He paused to take a breath and asked, "What are you doing in our trailer?"

"How many, son?" Joe asked.

"Five!"

"Five? All by yourself?" Joe was shocked.

"YESSSS!" he screamed. "All by myself!"

"YAAK!" Peter said. He was also visiting in the trailer.

"UGGG!" Joan added. "They stink!"

"Put them on the counter," Ann said.

"Are you going to clean them by yourself?" Joe asked.

"Yes." Edward got his Swiss knife from his packsack in the corner.

Peter asked, "Can I help? Huh?"

"No. They're Edward's fish," Ann said. "Leave him be. And watch how it's done."

Holding the fish down, Edward carefully cut off their heads. William showed him the right way at the creek. But Edward already knew; Joe showed him the day he saw the pirate.

"YAAK!" Peter said again.

"UGGG!" Joan added. "Look at the mess!"

Edward began to feel like the room had too many eyes. "Mom, tell Peter and Joan to leave me alone."

"Someone at the door for you, Edward," Joe said. "If this keeps up, the whole reunion will be in here."

Edward made faces at the Peter and Joan.

"Hello, Troy. Yup. I caught five fish. See."

"Edward has guts all over the place," Joan said.

"Oh, be quiet and leave him alone," Ann said.

When someone else banged at the trailer door, Joe said, "Good gracious. Who is it this time?"

"I heard Edward caught some fish," Todd said. "Can I see?"

"Sure," Joe said. "The whole campsite might as well see."

Edward held up a cleaned fish. "See."

Before too long, the room was full of people. "UGG," someone said. "What a stink. Phew." They all held their noses. They watched as Edward cut from the neck up the belly then put his thumb in and...

"YAAAK!" Joan said.

"UGGG!" Peter said.

"UGGG...YAAK!" the kids said together. "Look at all the blood and guts."

But it didn't bother Edward. Soon the fish were all cleaned and rinsed and the remains placed in a garbage bag. His foster mom even let him cook them himself.

And Edward was sure hungry after his trip in the woods.

He put several pats of butter in the heated frying pan. Then, after turning the fish over several times in flour, he placed them in the hot butter.

The sizzle in the pan cooked the fish just right. They really smelled good. Everyone's eyes grew larger and larger.

Joe, Ann, and all the visitors kept looking at the frying pan. And watched Edward take the pan from the stove.

They saw him put the fish on his plate.

When he looked up, watching eyes were replaced by smacking lips. He knew they were just trying to tease him.

Edward put a napkin under his chin. Then he held up his fork and knife and said, "Wow! All mine!"

Then the voices became loud noises. "Edward! Edward! Can I have a piece?"

Joan said, "Me, too." So did Peter and Todd.

Should he share his fish?

"Me, too." "Can I?" "Meee, too." Their voices were like ocean waves slapping at the shore, surrounding him.

These were the same people who were full of "UGGGS" and "YAKKS." *How come they changed their minds?* Their eyes were almost pleading. Edward could feel their hearts beating faster and faster.

"MEE too. MEE too," sounded like the beating of drums.

Should I give everyone a piece? he wondered. *Should I?* Thoughts flew around like buzzing mosquitoes. Edward looked up at his foster mom and foster dad. They weren't making it any easier.

It was his decision.

Ann was smiling. Joe was chewing on his thumb.

Edward finally decided to share. He made sure each person had a piece of fish. Satisfied "AAHS!" and "YUMS!" now filled the room.

Everything was so funny that he giggled a lot and fell on the floor. There was just no way he could stop. Maybe it was because his feet were tired from the long hike.

Or because his arms were tired from all the casts he made.

But he was happy. All the kids were, too, even his foster mom and dad. By now, everyone was giggling and laughing. As they stood around, he felt like a fish in a pond.

Edward looked up at Joan. He wasn't upset with her anymore.

She gave him a huge, seven-year-old smile then held up the last piece of trout before it disappeared into her mouth. "Yum...yum," she said. "Okay if I call you my cousin?"

Now Edward was really happy. It was like being part of the family.

"Sure," he said, with a smile that easily matched hers.

Chapter 13: Not So Fast, You

Back in Truro, things began to change. By now, everyone was calling Edward "Wish." It wasn't because he was skinny, like a wishbone. Maybe it was because he was always wishing for something. And he knew if he kept wishing, he would be adopted someday.

Right now, though, he had other things on his mind.

"We're going on this hike, young fellow. So shake it."

When your foster dad spoke impatiently, you better listen. And you better not call him Joe, either, when he was in this mood.

That was almost an hour ago. Now Edward was tripping over his own feet and his toes were sore. That's what happened when you had two left feet.

"He's not used to all these outings. Give him a break," his foster mom said before they left.

"Ann, he's beginning to toughen up. I want him to come on these hikes. Come on, Wish. Remember how much fun you had at the reunion campfire?"

Edward nodded quietly.

"It's our last hike before hunting season. And then those guns will begin shooting."

"Wait up," Edward said.

"Why so slow? We can take a rest later. Come on, look

how beautiful it is out here."

"No...yes."

"Well, what is it?"

Are you angry with me? Edward almost asked. Looking at the ground, he noticed his new boots were all muddy. And his pants were wet from stomping on the old road.

He wished Grandpa Jim were here right now. "No. It's just..."

"Do you think I'm too tough on you, Edward?"

Edward hoped his foster dad couldn't read his thoughts. "No...well, yes."

"What is it?"

Edward looked at a large maple and tried to forget his squishy socks. Should he tell Joe his feet were freezing?

His foster dad walked ahead quickly. "Try and catch up if you can," he shouted back. Then, like magic, Joe disappeared up the trail.

Edward stood alone with his thoughts. His fists clenched and unclenched. Darn. Darn. He was too upset to even yell. He leaned against a tree.

Now he felt like a fallen hazelnut. *Maybe a squirrel will find me. Then hide me,* he thought. That would stop grouchy Joe. He'd probably kick butt then, if Edward went missing.

Sounds arrived at his ears like whispers. He didn't realize the trees were just scraping their limbs together in a nervous dance.

Water was rushing somewhere.

His eyes grew large as his imagination saw things that weren't really there. His blond head felt sweaty under the tight cap.

Edward could easily have started screaming.

With Joe, it was okay. But with only him, it was terror-time. He had to get going and find out what his foster dad was up to. Was he playing a game? It wasn't funny.

"Dad!" No answer. "DADDD!" He hoped Joe didn't mind being screamed at or being called "Dad," either.

The trail ahead turned to the left, and Edward followed slowly, almost stumbling. "Dad. DA-AD!" He came to a fork. Now what to do? There were no tracks, only sloppy water. Something passed this way. Yes, there. Were those Joe's tracks?

Maybe some other person came by not too long ago. He didn't know what to do next. *Which one? Make up your mind. Come on, Edward.* He knew Joe was waiting impatiently somewhere.

He turned left. The trail took him farther past the main trail. It just went on and on.

His feet were tired. Stomach rumbles said, "Time to eat." With cold fingers, he found his knapsack and opened it. Egg sandwiches made him feel much better.

Joe said a walk in the woods gave you an appetite. Why did he always have to drag Edward along anyway? So, where was his foster dad now?

"DAADDD!" Still there was no answer. His cry was lost in the trees. After hiking for a while, Edward sat down.

A movement caught his eye. *White, no, it's grey. A bunny.* "It's a bunny!" Losing his balance, he fell on his stomach, hands grabbing at the leafy carpet. Edward studied the rabbit's quick movements, feeling happy even though he mashed his face on the wet ground.

His heart hammered. A real live wild rabbit! If only his foster dad could see him now.

So he wouldn't frighten the little creature, he became

very still. The rabbit hopped around the fallen apples spread around the tree, sniffing and nibbling.

The fluffy ball of fur had a black tinge around his eyes. Almost like a bank robber.

"Please don't run away," Edward said. "Be my friend." But the little animal didn't stay for long. When it hopped away to new territory, Edward felt cold and alone. Maybe the rabbit didn't want him for a friend after all.

He shuffled to his feet and wiped away the wet leaves. Joe should be back soon. At least Edward's stomach was full from his snack. Good thing he had his Swiss knife along, too.

He came to a clearing beside the worn trail and sat on a fallen log. A large willow branch looked inviting. *I'll carve my initials,* Edward thought. As he picked at the bark with his blade, he sensed a pair of eyes watching from nearby.

Edward turned around and stared into the startled face of a deer, still as a statue beside a fir tree. Animal ears stretched wide and alert.

He bit his lip and scrunched his fingers together. Just a few minutes ago, his legs felt nothing but tired. Now energy raced through them.

He tingled all over. A real live deer brought forward such a feeling. Right here. Now. He barely whispered, "Oh...oh."

His lips moved with the word, "Beautiful." His cheeks were on fire. "Awesome," he whispered. He must not move. "Be careful. Don't scare it," his senses said. And the deer just stood there looking at Edward. There was no fear in his searching look.

Suddenly, Edward saw with horror a hunter standing

not more than a hundred feet behind the deer. He was aiming a rifle in his direction. Was he going to shoot? Oh no, no. Edward barely moved. If he did, the deer might try to run and maybe get shot.

His mind formed a plan. If he stayed still, the deer hunter might not shoot because Edward was in the way. Was he brave enough to stay still?

Would the hunter give up and go away?

Edward was just a kid, and his foster dad would think this was stupid. Maybe this was a dangerous idea, just to save a deer. He hoped Joe would think he was brave. Maybe he shouldn't tell him. Then it would be his secret. He almost giggled.

For some reason, the deer couldn't see the danger.

Maybe it was because he could trust a boy to keep him from harm. That's exactly what kept the deer alive. As long as Edward stayed in the line of fire, the hunter would not shoot.

Edward saw the anger on the stranger's face as he lowered his rifle. Suddenly, another noise interrupted the waiting game going on.

"Edward! Edward!"

As Joe stepped into the clearing, the deer turned and leaped into the forest. And safety.

"Hey, kid, what did you do that for? Brat!" the stranger shouted. Edward stood quietly, head hanging.

He could see the confusion on Joe's face. Would Edward be able to explain what he did? Would his foster dad understand? It wasn't just so he could be brave. It was more than that.

The deer needed him. And for the first time it felt good. Someone needed the wimp.

His foster dad and the hunter went off to the side. One voice came across loudly. "You're nothing but a rotten poacher. You scared my son!" Edward could hardly believe his ears. His foster dad said, "Son!"

It sounded great.

"I'm contacting the RCMP and the game warden about this!" Joe shouted. After a moment, the hunter went off, mumbling to himself.

Edward stood still as his foster dad came to him. He could feel those eyes burning into his. Joe had a mean look. "Naggy" and "grouch" were words that disappeared from his vocabulary right then.

This man looked like he was ready to zap Edward.

Did he really want to call this guy Dad?

He could almost guess the questions to come. "Why didn't you let the hunter shoot the deer?" Or "How come you did something so dangerous?" And even, "What a stupid thing to do."

Edward felt tears trickle down his cheeks. He was like a balloon ready to burst. He needed someone right now. He wanted his foster dad to hug him tightly. He felt alone and helpless.

Joe stood before him, shaking his head. Edward tried to read his thoughts. His face didn't look so mean now.

Mr. Lawrence, he wanted to say. *I love you so much. Why don't you love me?* But he couldn't. Something always held him back.

Joe stared back at him. Edward imagined what he looked like—a few tears dribbling down his cheek like a baby. He also knew his jeans were ripped. How much for a new pair?

Edward even had mud caked on his chest. And his

winter jacket was full of thistles.

His foster dad just stood there, shaking his head, smiling now.

Smiling?

Magic words made Edward's heart race wildly. "I love you, too, son." Tears rushed down Mr. Lawrence's face, but Edward didn't care.

Joe needed him right now.

Chapter 14: Getting it Right

An early snowfall surprised them as they headed back. This time it was Edward who said, "Let's hurry, before the snow gets too deep."

"Yeah. Good idea," Joe answered. "I'll go first. That will make it easier for you. Follow in my trail, okay?"

"Cool," Edward answered. He followed exactly as he was instructed. He carefully placed each step in Joe's footprint.

"How's school?" Joe suddenly asked.

Edward knew this would come up. Going to school every day was bad enough. Talking about it on a weekend hike was even worse. He had a hard time getting along with the other kids in grade four.

They teased him because he was a foster kid. Maybe someone would adopt him one day. He hoped it would be the Lawrences, but nothing was being said about it.

The only thing he knew was happening was that the Children's Aid worker smiled a lot each time she made a home visit.

"You're doing okay?" Joe asked.

"School is okay," Edward answered.

"Then how come your math and English is in trouble, chum?"

Aha! The trap was sprung, and Edward fell for it.

"I don't want to talk about it now, okay?" He wished he didn't say that. He came here to have fun.

The snow was soft and fluffy, and the wind blew sharply against his face. Good thing he listened to Ann and brought a scarf.

"Keep lifting your feet higher," Joe said. "That way you won't trip on a branch under the snow."

Edward was tired of his foster dad always telling him to watch out for this. Or watch out for that. Like a general giving orders.

"Cross the street carefully." "Keep an eye out for the train when you cross the tracks." And it went on and on. Who did he think he was, his father or something?

"Can we rest?" Edward asked.

"Already tuckered out?" Joe teased.

Always trying to get my blood boiling, Edward thought. *When will he ever stop? When I grow up I'll move so far away, I'll—*

"Watch out!"

But it was too late.

As they were ducking under some branches, his foster dad let one go, and it smacked Edward in the face.

He fell backwards into the snow, and his ankle twisted sideways. Now that really hurt.

At first, Joe was angry. Then he began to laugh but stopped when Edward let out a yell. The pounding in the boy's head wouldn't stop. Punching at the snow didn't help, either.

"Oh, great," Joe said, shaking his head.

Then he bent down and picked Edward up. "Gosh, you're heavy."

It's been a long time since I ever got carried, Edward

thought.

His foster dad placed Edward sitting up, back against a tree. Then he started digging out snow in a large circle. "For a fire," Joe said before Edward asked any questions. "You sit there, and I'll get you a log to sit on."

Before too long, Edward was snug on a log. A fire was going, and some of the numbness was leaving his fingers and toes.

"You make a good fire, Mr. Lawrence." Edward tried to smile.

"I know I'm kind of tough on you sometimes," Joe said.

"Sort of," Edward mumbled.

"How do you mean, son?"

He keeps calling me "son," Edward thought. "You pick on me a lot." There, he said it. Would his foster dad be upset?

"I know I do."

He knows he does? "Well, not all the time..." Edward tried to be kind.

"Let's look at that ankle." Joe took Edward's foot, removed the boot and sock then felt his ankle and toes. He held the small foot between both of his bare hands to give it maximum warmth.

"Feels better already. And the fire helps a lot," Edward said.

After ringing out the sock, Joe carefully put the boot back on.

Both man and boy said nothing for a while. Edward watched the flames lick at the wood. His foster dad began to put on larger deadwood picked from fallen spruce.

"Aren't you hungry?" Edward asked.

Joe pulled out his thermos of hot chocolate and

poured Edward and himself a cup. Then he brought out aluminium foil packages of food and placed them on the hot coals.

"Yes, I'm starved," Joe finally answered.

Edward looked around the forest. Tall trees nearly blocked out the sky, and patches of blue peeked back. The smoke from the fire hurt his eyes, but it didn't matter.

It was good sitting here. No one else was around, just the two of them. Edward liked it. "Dad?" he asked quietly. It felt comfortable saying the word "dad."

"What, son?"

Edward's blue eyes were a little moist. Maybe he was breathing too much smoke.

"Do you like that parka Ann bought you? I knew it would be warm enough. Am I right?"

"Dad..." Edward began again. He wished Mr. Lawrence would be quiet, for even a few minutes. Words were trying to force themselves up, right from the bottom of his stomach.

"What is it, Edward? Spit it out."

This time, Edward was more forceful. "I'm trying to say something. Please be quiet."

Then Joe began to laugh. "Imagine sitting on your wet behind and scolding me. What is it?"

"I just want to ask you..." Edward hesitated. His legs felt cold now. But that didn't matter. Words could not be held back any longer. They spilled from his lips like falling snow.

It brought a special smile from Mr. Lawrence when Edward asked, "Okay if I call you 'Dad' from now on?"

Chapter 15: Finding Each Other

Sunday was such a beautiful day that Ann insisted they go for a walk in Victoria Park. "And so convenient," she said, "just across the street."

"Thanks, Mom, my legs are still tired from our hike yesterday." Wish was happy to be living with foster parents who enjoyed the outdoors. "When is Joe coming, Mom?" He looked back at the house. This was the third time he checked.

He and his mom couldn't stand around forever. His legs twitched and itched to move forward. He couldn't complain, though, because Joe was older and maybe more tired than Edward felt.

He was pleased that Ann suggested this outing.

Finally, a familiar red cap and hunting jacket came into view. Joe's wire-rimmed glasses mirrored a smile. "Getting impatient?"

"Yeah, well...no," Edward stammered. "We're not going hunting, you know." He gave Joe a jab on the shoulder. "I bet you're worn out from yesterday's hike."

He was getting to like Joe more each day. Almost as much as Mom, even though Joe could be such a grouch.

"Okay then, let's have a little rest."

"What?" Edward mumbled under his breath. They barely started down the trail. Words became louder as sounds snuck out. "I'm not tired. Let's go on..." His voice dragged, but he kept hoping. "MOM!"

"No, Edward. Let's sit." They did. "After all," Mom said, "Joe is more tired than he will admit."

Edward looked around at the trees. They were all jingly from the wind. Then colours came into focus. Gold with orange and a reddish tinge created a beautiful autumn sight.

"What kind of tree is that, Dad?"

"A sugar maple."

"The one over there?" Ann said.

"A pine, I think. A red pine." Edward was proud of his knowledge. "Is that a Scotch pine?"

"Yes. You remembered." Then Joe jumped to his feet. "Ready?"

But Edward had many more questions. "Just one more?"

"Later."

"Look! A rabbit!" Edward shouted. At the sound of his voice, the small animal disappeared into the underbrush.

"Did you see the colours on the rabbit?" Joe asked.

"Yeah."

"What were they?"

"He was brown, and his feet had lots of white."

"Good. The colours are his camouflage. When snow comes, the rabbit will be white all over."

"Really?"

"Yes," Joe said.

"Cool."

"You're very observant, Edward. The rabbit was moving quite rapidly. I didn't think you'd see the white on the feet."

This made Edward feel really good. He liked hearing Joe saying nice things about him.

Oh, sure, his foster mom always did. But mom's have to, he convinced himself. Since Grandpa Jim went to Heaven, it was up to Mom to be his cheerleader.

I wonder if Mr. and Mrs. Lawrence ever talked about adopting me? he thought. The question was always on his mind. And he never wanted it to go away.

"I'm hungry," Edward said.

"Spoken like a true hiker," Joe said.

They ate delicious cream of broccoli soup from their thermos. Ann brought out the dessert: cookies and granola bars.

"Mom makes great soup," Edward boasted.

"You really love your foster mom, don't you?" Joe asked.

Edward's answer was a radiant smile as he looked in her direction. "I really feel comfortable calling her Mom," he said. "I'm glad you let me call you Dad, too."

Not too far down the trail, a young doe stood watching. "OHHH!" Edward gasped. The noise startled the wild animal. It turned quickly and leaped into the woods. Its white tail bobbed like a flag. Then it was gone.

"Was it afraid of me?" Edward asked.

"No," Joe answered.

"Did I scare it?"

"Yes."

"How come?"

"Nature tells it to be very careful around humans," Ann said quietly.

"Why?"

"Because we might hurt it," the man said, nodding

solemnly.

"But it's not deer season," Edward said. "Besides, hunters aren't allowed in this park."

"I know, but each wild animal still has to be careful."

The boy thought for a moment then asked, "Dad, how come people kill things?"

"Some hunt to eat the game. I prefer to use a camera in the woods and get some exercise."

"Me, too," Ann said.

The boy nodded in understanding.

"It also gives me a chance to spend some time with you," Joe added. He placed his hand on the boy's shoulder. "That's how I get to know you better."

Imagine, the "grouch" wanted to know Edward better.

The rest of the day was a challenge. It rained tiny pellets of hail. The weather drove the adults and boy into the shelter of the trees, where white birch gleamed like smiling teeth.

When the hail stopped, they walked more trails, their boots scuffing across rocky sections. "These small stones are picked up by partridge in early morning and early evening," Joe explained.

"Why?" the boy asked.

"It goes into a crop, like a packsack under their throat. It helps break up the leaves that are swallowed."

"Oh."

Then they heard a pounding sound. It was as if a small child was banging on a log faster and faster with a stick. The pattern reached a high pitch that rose through the trees.

"It's beautiful," Edward said. "What is it?"

"A male partridge calling for a mate. It's the pattern of

life, Edward."

"The same as how we all came into this world," Ann piped up.

"Yeah...I know," the boy answered. "Grandpa talked to me about babies and all that."

"He did?" Joe and Ann asked at the same time, eyebrows raised.

Their return trip was without conversation. Each had much to think about.

When they finally reached their home, Edward paused. He scratched his face and stretched then looked around. Dark clouds piled like pillows over the trees.

"Dad...Mom, I had an awesome time. When can we all go out again?" Edward asked.

He saw how his foster parents smiled at each other.

Chapter 16: Saying Good-Bye

Moving day came to Edward's house. He felt very sad having to leave his friends.

"Mom, can I go say goodbye?"

"What's that, Edward?"

Ann was packing dishes, and this was not a good time to bother her. But he had to ask.

"I have to say goodbye to my friends."

"I thought you already did. Several times, in fact."

"I know...but...just one more time?"

"All right, go ahead, but be back by one o'clock. Don't forget. What time?"

"One o'clock."

"You have your watch on. Good," she said.

Edward wondered what was so special about one o'clock.

He went to John's house. They had so much fun making snow forts. And he was a good snowball thrower, too.

No luck, no one home. How come?

He went down the street to say goodbye to Stephen. They had a fight once. But then they became good pals.

"Hi, Edward. I bet you're looking for your friend," Stephen's mom said.

"Yup." He gave his best smile. His hair kind of flopped

over his ears. Mom said he needed a haircut.

"Not here, Edward. He went out with his father somewhere."

"Oh, shucks, Mrs. Wasson. I'm moving today and…it's okay, I guess."

He went to Mrs. Lake's house. Stephanie should be home. Her mother was a painter who created beautiful art scenes of Victoria Park.

He liked to climb Stephanie's tree house by rope. "A ladder is too easy," she used to say. But Stephanie wasn't in, either.

Mrs. Lake said, "She went to her swimming class."

Edward went around the other side of the block. "I have to say goodbye to Ace," he said to the blue sky.

The sun smiled on Edward's freckles.

He heard a familiar bark down the street, so Edward hurried to pat the friendly black dog.

But Edward couldn't find Ace. The barking grew fainter and fainter. "Hey! This way, here, boy!"

It was no use. Ace was going in the other direction. "I wish I could hug Ace one more time," he said to the maple tree.

Edward headed for the park. He watched boys and girls having fun in the playground. If only he had one more chance to slide, swing high, and join in the soccer game.

The pool in Victoria Park used to be so chilly. *I'll miss the high diving board, too,* he thought.

"Will Spunky the lifeguard miss me?" He kicked at the grass. Edward couldn't see any of his friends. It was discouraging.

What about bushy Red the squirrel? Each time

Edward had a picnic with his foster mom and dad, Red came by. He would run down the tree and grab the bread then scoot back up again.

But Red wasn't around today.

Even the crows that followed him on the bike trails were gone, too. Their shrieks and cries were missing from the sky today.

Edward headed back home. His shoulders were slumped. It was almost one o'clock anyway. His watch said two minutes left.

So, he began to run.

Mom said to be home at one o'clock.

"I wonder why," he said to the baseball park. He ran faster. Edward's feet hit the pavement, like thunder.

He came roaring around the corner and suddenly stopped.

Just ahead of him was a large crowd of people. At his house! And children were hanging around the barbecue.

Hot dog and hamburger smells called to him.

Someone yelled, "Wish!" It was John.

John's here at my house? But why?

As Edward got closer, he spotted Stephen in the crowd. But didn't he go somewhere with his dad? *No, he's here, too.*

When Edward got closer, Stephanie ran forward. "Hurry up, Wish, we're all waiting for you."

"For me...?" Edward stammered.

"Yes, hurry. We're ready to eat. Where did you go?" He let Stephanie take his hand and pull him along.

As soon as the rest of the crowd saw him, they began to sing. "Happy Birthday to you! Happy Birthday to you!"

"OMIGOSH, a surprise birthday party!" he shouted. He

thought everyone forgot he was nine years old today.

Ace ran forward and jumped on his chest. Edward rubbed under the dog's chin. Then he bent down and gave Ace a big hug.

By now, his cheeks were getting wet.

Happy tears were impossible to hold back. He felt choked up. The whole neighbourhood was here.

Suddenly, Mom and Dad were by his side.

"We wanted to surprise you, son. I knew it would be hard for you to move away. Especially on your birthday." Mom gave him a mother-bear hug. Dad gave him a father-bear hug.

Everyone had a great time, munching treats and drinking pop. They were laughing and running and talking all at once.

It was a great goodbye party.

Even Spunky the lifeguard came.

High up in his maple tree, bushy Red chattered happily.

Edward looked up and gave the best goodbye smile he could. "Bye, Red," he whispered.

"Bye, sky. Bye, trees. Bye, house."

Then Edward, the boy everyone knew as Wish, put up his hand. And everyone stopped talking and looked towards the boy. "I have an announcement to...make."

He choked back tears as he looked around. Then he said, "I'm getting adopted by the Lawrences!"

At first, there were thunderous cheers then happy tears when everyone heard the good news.

And the best part was when Wish ran to his new parents.

Chapter 17: A New Beginning

Edward was tired. His curly hair danced in the wind, and his muscles ached. How come his dad asked him to lift such heavy things?

"You're a big part of this family now, so help as much as possible," Mom also said.

The suitcase rubbed against his leg.

Just two weeks ago, they came to look at the house for the final time. Then they bought it.

The blue vinyl siding looked really neat. But it had only a small back yard.

"This is so heavy. I hate moving. It's too much work."

It was great being adopted, now that the official papers were signed. His wishing did come true. Edward knew Grandpa Jim was so happy for him.

He really loved being part of a family again. And having such a nice mom and dad. "Now we have to get this stuff in our new house." He still talked to himself.

"Edward, hurry up, please."

There goes Dad again. Edward used to think he was so mean. But he really wasn't.

"Edward. Hurry up...please."

"Mom! I heard you." Where was she? Maybe she'd make him a hot chocolate. "Whoops. No hot chocolate." The food was still in the van.

He struggled up the second floor steps and entered his room. "This is all mine," he said to the empty space. Edward lifted up the window and something black rushed across the yard.

"Whoa! Was that a black squirrel?"

He ran downstairs into the back yard. Then he walked slowly around two maple trees and looked up. No, he saw nothing, nothing at all.

"Mom? Did you see that?"

"What, dear?" his mother asked through the screen window. He wished she would take a rest. "Lots more to carry," she said.

His dad could lift heavy things like the movers. He had huge muscles and liked to show them off. Edward didn't want to wear out his own muscles.

"Mom, did you see that black shadow?"

"Oh honey, we don't have time right now. Come and give me a hand with the rest."

Just then, he saw the cat for the first time. It was black and shaggy with bright green eyes and large feet. The cat walked sort of like a shaggy buffalo, so low to the ground it looked like its belly was dragging.

"Mom, look!"

She did, but...too late. "I'm sorry, son. Missed it."

The shadow was gone. "What a cool name. Shadow."

His mom agreed.

The rest of his day was filled with grunts and scrapes. He was sweaty. His shirt clung to his back.

"Edward!"

There's Dad again. Gosh, every time I'm thinking, he's bothering me.

"Did you see a black, furry thing in the back yard?

Looked like a walking rug. Ha, ha, ha."

Dad was always teasing. *He must have overheard me talking to Mom.* "Very funny, Dad," Edward said under his breath. "NOOO...it was a cat, a big, shaggy cat. I'm calling him Shadow."

"Oh, you have a new friend, do you?" his father said as he joined him by the tree.

"Sure." Edward loved cats. He always wanted one. "Hey, maybe...gee, what an idea. Dad!"

"Now, Edward, for goodness' sake. Are you going to help or not?"

"Yes, Dad, but..."

"Edward, later...please."

"Dad...okay." *Back to work, I guess.* As Edward turned to go, "darn" slipped out.

"Watch the mouth, Edward. No complaining."

"I'm coming, Dad."

That night, the wind whistled through his bedroom screen. Edward was certain it was Shadow he heard calling. He lay on his mattress in his sleeping bag, thinking.

Meows continued to drift up to his second story bedroom. Was Shadow lonely? Edward wished the cat was right here beside him.

"Maybe I can pretend. Even if Mom and Dad don't let me, I can pretend he's mine." But what if he was someone else's?

Thoughts of another boy somewhere down the block entered his mind. "I wonder how my cat is?" that little boy might be saying right now.

Unable to settle down, Edward turned and twisted on his mattress.

Dad told him it was always hard to sleep in a strange bed. But this was only a temporary bed. His proper one was in parts, stacked in one corner of the room.

Maybe he couldn't sleep because of the move. And the friends he left behind. He hoped he would get used to it soon.

"Edward?" Mom rapped at the door. "Talking in your sleep again?"

"No, Mom."

"May I come in?"

"Sure."

"I forgot to tuck you in, son."

"Is Dad downstairs? Will he come tuck me in, too?"

"Sure. He understands even big boys like to be tucked in."

"Mom, can I ask you somethin'? I don't think Dad would...but anyway..."

"What is it, son?"

"I wish I could keep Shadow."

Then he told his mom the games he and his friend would play. Maybe Edward could be Shadow's foster parent. Or even adopt him, just like he was adopted.

Suddenly, Dad was in the room beside them. And Edward went over his request again.

"Sleep on it, son. But I'll make a deal with you..."

"We know how much you want a cat," Mom added.

"Lots of room here for a cat." Dad smiled.

Edward felt his heart pounding. It was hard to get to sleep now. They agreed to put an ad in the paper the next day.

Before anyone could say "Shadow" fifty times, someone phoned. "I'm so glad you found my cat" was all

Edward remembered.

It was hard to point out his friend Shadow, who hung around the back yard. When the owner called, "Frisky," the black cat ran forward. Not "Shadow" but "Frisky."

That night, over a delicious meal of chicken, Edward thought about the past few days.

Shadow was home. It hurt, but that's where he knew Shadow belonged. His master looked so happy to have him back.

Just like this was where Edward belonged. He looked around the table. Mom and Dad were watching him closely.

They knew how much he loved that cat. It was hard to let him go. "It's okay, Mom. It's okay, Dad."

It was not easy to say the other words out loud. "I know this is where I belong. And Shadow is where he belongs."

Now he had two parents who loved him very much.

And there was a best part.

He didn't have to be called "Wish" anymore.

Also from InkSpotter Publishing

Backless, Strapless & Slit to the Throat
Collywobblers
The Communal Desk
Family Lines
Holiday Writes
Paper Wings

http://inkspotter.com/bookstore

AND COMING SOON

Breaking Free
Wait a Minute, I Have to Take Off My Bra
Writing the Bottom Line

http://inkspotter.com/publications/books